CHRISTMAS COOKING

Rebecca Gilpin and Catherine Atkinson

Edited by Fiona Watt
Designed by Amanda Gulliver
Photographs by Howard Allman
Illustrated by Kim Lane and Sue Stitt

Managing Designer: Mary Cartwright
With thanks to Katrina Fearn and Brian Voakes
American Editor: Carrie Seay

Contents

2 Little Christmas trees
4 Coconut mice
6 Cheesy Christmas stars
8 Creamy chocolate fudge
10 Crinkly Christmas pies
12 Painted cookies
14 Starry jam tart
16 Peppermint creams
18 Shortbread
20 Chocolate truffles
22 Shining star cookies
24 Snowmen and presents
26 Iced gingerbread hearts
28 Christmas tree cupcakes
30 Wrapping ideas
32 Tags and ribbons

Little Christmas trees

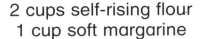

You could arrange the presents around the trees.

To make 10 trees and 16 presents, you will need:

2 cups self-rising flour
1 cup soft margarine
4 tablespoons of milk
1 level teaspoon of baking powder
1 cup sugar
2-3 drops vanilla extract
4 medium eggs

For the butter icing:
$\frac{2}{3}$ cup butter, softened
$2\frac{1}{2}$ cups powdered sugar
1 teaspoon of vanilla extract
food dyes

Heat the oven to 350°F, before you start.

Use a 13 x 9 inch baking pan.

Use a paper towel to wipe oil on the pan.

Use a wooden spoon.

1. Draw around a pan on greaseproof paper. Cut it out. Wipe oil inside the pan. Put the paper into the pan, and grease it.

2. Sift the flour into a large mixing bowl. Add the margarine, milk, baking powder, sugar and vanilla extract.

3. Break the eggs into a small bowl. Beat them with a fork. Add them to the flour mixture. Beat everything together well.

Make trunks for the trees from chocolate bars or cookies.

The cake should be springy when you press it. Be careful, as it will be hot.

4. Spoon the mixture into the pan. Smooth the top. Bake it in the oven for 40-45 minutes, until the middle is springy.

5. Leave the cake in the pan to cool, then lift it out. Put the butter into a bowl. Beat it with a wooden spoon until it is creamy.

6. Sift in the powdered sugar. Stir it in, a little at a time. Stir in the vanilla. Put three-quarters of the icing in a bowl.

To make the color stronger, add more dye, a drop at a time.

—These will be the presents.

7. Mix in a little green food dye. Divide the rest of the icing into three bowls. Mix a drop of food dye into each one.

8. Cut a strip 3in. wide from one end of the cake. Cut it into 16 small squares. Cut the cake in half along its length.

9. Cut out ten triangles. Ice them with green icing. Ice the presents with the colored icing. Press candy onto the cakes.

Decorate the trees with candy.

Coconut mice

To make about eight large mice, five medium mice and three baby mice, you will need:

2 cups powdered sugar, sifted
1 cup condensed milk
3 cups shredded coconut
red food dye
candy for ears
silver cake decorating balls
red licorice strings

1. Mix the powdered sugar and the condensed milk in a bowl. Mix in the coconut. Put the mixture into two bowls.

2. Add a few drops of red dye to each bowl and mix it in. Then add a few more drops of dye to one of the bowls.

For baby mice, use a teaspoon for the body.

4

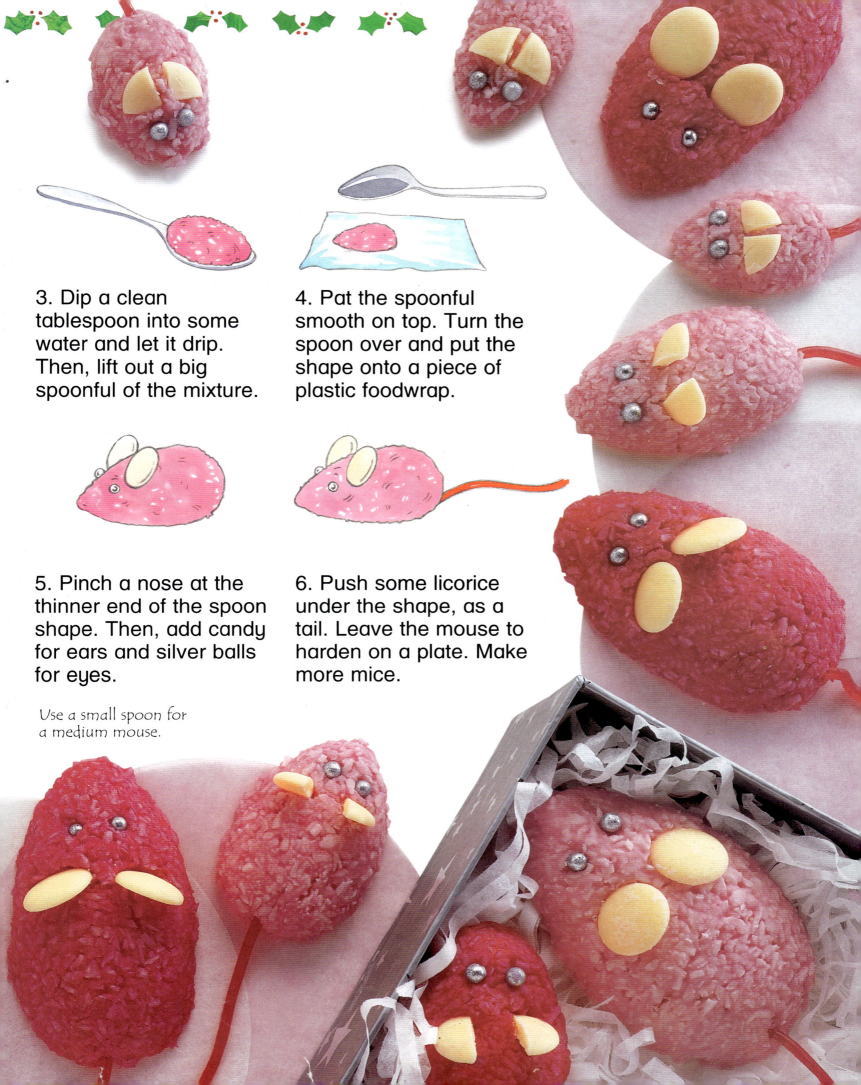

3. Dip a clean tablespoon into some water and let it drip. Then, lift out a big spoonful of the mixture.

4. Pat the spoonful smooth on top. Turn the spoon over and put the shape onto a piece of plastic foodwrap.

5. Pinch a nose at the thinner end of the spoon shape. Then, add candy for ears and silver balls for eyes.

6. Push some licorice under the shape, as a tail. Leave the mouse to harden on a plate. Make more mice.

Use a small spoon for a medium mouse.

Cheesy Christmas stars

To make about 25 stars, you will need:
1¼ cups self-rising flour
½ teaspoon salt
¼ cup margarine
²∕₃ cup cheese, finely grated
1 egg and 2 tablespoons of milk, beaten together
star-shaped cutter
greased cookie sheet

Heat the oven to 400°F, before you start.

1. Sift the flour and salt through a sieve. Add the margarine and rub it with your fingers to make fine crumbs.

2. Leave a tablespoon of the grated cheese on a saucer. Add the rest of the cheese to the bowl and stir it in.

3. Put a tablespoon of the beaten egg and milk mixture into a cup. Mix the rest into the flour to make a dough.

Use a rolling pin.

Use a pastry brush.

4. Sprinkle flour onto a clean work surface. Roll out the dough, until it is slightly thinner than your little finger.

5. Use the cutter to cut out star shapes. Cut them close together. Make the scraps into a ball, and roll them out.

6. Cut out more stars. Brush the stars with the rest of the egg mixture, then sprinkle them with the rest of the cheese.

7. Put the stars onto the greased cookie sheet. Bake them in the oven for eight to ten minutes, until they are golden.

These stars are delicious to eat when they are warm.

Creamy chocolate fudge

To make about 36 squares of fudge, you will need:
½ cup full-fat cream cheese
1 level tablespoon cocoa powder
1½ cups powdered sugar
1 teaspoon of cooking oil, for greasing
½ cup semi-sweet chocolate chips
2 tablespoons butter
a shallow square cake or brownie pan
greaseproof paper

Find out how to wrap
pieces of fudge on page 30.

Use a pencil to draw around the pan.

1. Put the cream cheese into a bowl. Sift the cocoa and powdered sugar into the bowl too. Mix them together well.

2. Put the cake pan onto a sheet of greaseproof paper and draw around it. Cut out the shape, just inside the line.

3. Use a paper towel to wipe oil onto the sides and base of the pan. Press in the paper square and wipe it too.

4. Melt the chocolate and butter as in steps 1-3 on page 20. Then, stir in a tablespoon of the cream cheese mixture.

5. Pour the chocolate into the cheese mixture in the bowl. Beat them together with a spoon until they are creamy.

6. Spoon the mixture into the pan, and push it into the corners. Make the top of the fudge as flat as you can.

7. Smooth the top with the back of a spoon. Put the pan in the refrigerator for two hours, or until the fudge is firm.

8. Use a blunt knife to loosen the edges of the fudge, then turn it out onto a large plate. Remove the paper.

9. Cut the fudge into lots of squares. Then, put the plate in the refrigerator for two hours, until the fudge is hard.

Crinkly Christmas pies

To make 12 pies, you will need:
4 apples
3 tablespoons orange juice or cold water
½ cup dried cranberries or raisins
2 teaspoons sugar
½ teaspoon ground cinnamon
14oz fillo dough (about 6 sheets)
2 tablespoons butter
2 tablespoons powdered sugar
twelve hole muffin tin

Heat the oven to 375°F, before you start.

You may need to ask someone to help you.

Put the lid back on after you've stirred the apples.

Stir the mixture often.

1. Peel the apples. Cut them into quarters and cut out the cores. Cut them into small pieces and put them in the pan.

2. Add the juice or water and put the pan on very low heat. Cover it with a lid. Cook for 20 minutes, stirring often.

3. Stir in the fruit, sugar and cinnamon. Cook the mixture for about five minutes, then take it off the heat.

Keep the six sheets together.

Use a pastry brush.

4. Take the pan off the heat. Unwrap the dough. Cut all the sheets into six squares. Cover them with foodwrap.

5. Put the butter in a small pan and melt it over a low heat. Brush a little butter over one of the dough squares.

6. Put the square into a hole in the tray, buttered side up. Press it gently into the hole. Brush butter onto another square.

Overlap the dough sheets so that they look like a star.

7. Put this square over the first one. Overlap the corners slightly. Butter and add a third square. Repeat in all the holes.

8. Put the tray on the middle shelf of the oven and cook for 10 minutes. Take it out and leave it to cool for five minutes.

Heat the apples until they bubble a little.

9. Take the pastry cases out of the tray and put them onto a large plate. Heat the apples again for about two minutes.

Eat the pies warm or cold.

10. Spoon the apple mixture into the pastry cases, so that they are almost full. Sift powdered sugar onto them.

Painted cookies

To make about 15 cookies, you will need:
½ cup powdered sugar
½ cup soft margarine
the yolk from a large egg
vanilla extract
1¼ cups flour
plastic foodwrap
big cookie cutters
greased cookie sheet

To decorate the cookies:
an egg yolk
food dyes

Heat the oven to 350°F,
before you start.

Use a wooden spoon.

1. Sift the powdered sugar through a sieve into a large bowl. Add the margarine. Mix well until they are smooth.

2. Add the large egg yolk and stir it in well. Then, add a few drops of vanilla extract. Stir the vanilla into the mixture.

3. Hold a sieve over the bowl and pour the flour into it. Sift the flour through the sieve, to remove any lumps.

4. Mix in the flour until you get a smooth dough. Wrap the dough in plastic foodwrap and put it in the freezer.

Decorate your cookies with lots of different patterns.

It takes time to decorate the cookies, so you could freeze some of the dough to use another day.

5. Put the egg yolk into a bowl and beat it with a fork. Put it onto saucers. Mix a few drops of food dye into each one.

6. Take the dough out of the freezer. Roll out half of it onto a floury work surface, until it is as thin as your little finger.

7. Press out shapes with cutters. Use a spatula to lift them onto a cookie sheet. Roll out the rest of the dough.

8. Cut out more shapes. Use a clean paintbrush to paint shapes on the cookies with the egg and dye mixture.

9. Bake the cookies for 10-12 minutes. Remove them from the oven. Let them cool a little, then lift them onto a wire rack.

Starry jam tart

To make one jam tart, you will need:
12oz ready-made pie-crust
about 2 tablespoons flour
6 rounded tablespoons seedless raspberry or
strawberry preserves
1 tablespoon milk
1 shallow pie tin
small star-shaped cutter

Heat the oven to 400°F, before you start.

You can use any shape of cutter you like. Stars and holly leaves look very Christmassy.

1. Take the dough out of the refrigerator and leave it for 10 minutes. Sprinkle a clean work surface with some flour.

2. Cut off a quarter of the dough and wrap it in some plastic foodwrap. Sprinkle some flour onto a rolling pin.

3. Roll out the bigger piece of dough. Turn it a little, then roll it again. Make a circle about 12in. across.

Sift a slice of tart with a little powdered sugar and serve it with whipped cream or ice cream.

4. Put the rolling pin at one side of the dough. Roll the dough around it and lift it up. Place it over the tin and unroll it.

The rolling pin cuts off the extra dough.

5. Dip a finger into some flour and press the dough into the edges of the tin. Then, roll the rolling pin across the top.

6. Spoon the preserves into the dough crust. Spread it out with the back of a spoon. Roll out the rest of the dough.

7. Using the cutter, cut out about 12 shapes. Brush them with a little milk and place them on top of the preserves.

The pastry should be golden brown.

8. Put the jam tart in the oven. Bake it for about 20 minutes. Take the tart from the oven and let the jam cool before serving.

Peppermint creams

To make about 25 peppermint creams, you will need:
2 cups powdered sugar
half the white of a small egg mixed from powdered egg
or powdered meringue
(mix as directed on container)
¼ teaspoon peppermint flavoring
1 tablespoon lemon juice
green food dye
rolling pin
small cutters
a cookie sheet covered in
plastic foodwrap

Put peppermint creams in boxes, to give as presents.

1. Sift the powdered sugar through a sieve into a large bowl. Make a hole in the middle of the sugar with a spoon.

2. Mix the egg white, peppermint flavoring and lemon juice in a small bowl. Pour the mixture into the sugar.

3. Use a blunt knife to stir the mixture. Then, squeeze it between your fingers until it is smooth, like a dough.

The powdered sugar stops the mixture from sticking.

4. Cut the mixture into two pieces. Put each piece into a bowl. Add a few drops of green food dye to one bowl.

5. Use your fingers to mix in the dye. If the mixture is sticky, add a little more powdered sugar and mix it in.

6. Sprinkle a little powdered sugar onto a clean work surface. Sprinkle some onto a rolling pin too.

Cut the
shapes close
together.

7. Roll out the green
mixture until it is about
as thick as your little
finger. Use cutters to cut
out lots of shapes.

8. Use a blunt knife to lift
the shapes onto the
cookie sheet. Roll out
the white mixture and
cut out more shapes.

9. Lift all the shapes
onto the cookie sheet.
Leave them for at least
an hour until they
become hard.

Shortbread

To make eight pieces, you will need:
butter for greasing
1½ cups flour
½ cup butter, refrigerated, cut into chunks
¼ cup sugar
an 8-inch shallow pan

Heat the oven to 300°F, before you start.

1. Grease the bottom and sides of the pan with some butter on a piece of paper towel. Make sure it is all greased.

2. Sift the flour through a sieve into a large bowl. Then, add the chunks of butter to the bowl too.

3. Mix in the butter so that it is coated in flour. Rub it into the flour with your fingers until it is like fine breadcrumbs.

4. Stir in the sugar with a wooden spoon. Hold the bowl with one hand and squeeze the mixture into a ball with the other.

5. Press the mixture into the pan with your fingers. Use the back of a spoon to smooth the top and make it level.

6. Use a fork to press patterns around the edge and holes in the middle. Cut the shortbread into eight pieces.

Shortbread makes an ideal present. See pages 30–31 for wrapping ideas.

7. Bake the shortbread for 30 minutes, until it is golden. After 10 minutes, take it out of the pan. Put it on a wire rack to cool.

Chocolate truffles

To make about 20 truffles, you will need:
1 cup semi-sweet chocolate chips
2 tablespoons butter
¼ cup powdered sugar
½ cup store-bought pound-cake or shortcake,
crumbled into fine crumbs
¼ cup finely grated coconut
¼ cup chocolate sprinkles
paper miniature candy cups

1. Pour water into a pan, until it is about 1 inch deep. Heat it until it bubbles, then remove the pan from the heat.

2. Put the chocolate drops and the butter into a heatproof bowl. Put on oven gloves and gently put the bowl in the pan.

Ask someone to help you to lift the bowl.

3. Stir the chocolate and butter together until they have melted. Using oven gloves, carefully lift the bowl out of the water.

4. Sift the powdered sugar through a sieve into the chocolate. Add the cake crumbs and stir until everything is well mixed.

The white truffles are covered with coconut.

5. Leave the mixture to cool. Then, put the coconut onto one plate, and the chocolate sprinkles onto another.

6. When the mixture is firm and thick, scoop some up with a spoon. Put the spoonful into the coconut or sprinkles.

Roll the spoonful to make a ball.

7. Roll the spoonful of chocolate around until it is covered, then put it in a candy cup. Make lots more truffles.

8. Put the truffles onto a large plate. Put the plate in the refrigerator for 30 minutes, or until the truffles are firm.

Shining star cookies

To make about 20 cookies, you will need:
½ cup soft brown sugar
⅓ cup soft margarine
half a small egg
1¼ cups flour
1 teaspoon allspice
hard candy, assorted flavors
large star-shaped cookie cutter
fat drinking straw
small round cookie cutter,
slightly bigger than the candy
large cookie sheet lined with baking parchment

Heat the oven to 350°F, before you start.

Thread thin ribbon through the holes.

1. Using a wooden spoon, mix the brown sugar and margarine really well, getting rid of any lumps in the mixture.

2. Break the egg into a separate bowl. Beat the egg with a fork until the yolk and the white are mixed together.

3. Mix half of the beaten egg into the mixture in the bowl, a little at a time. You don't need the other half.

4. Sift the flour and allspice through a sieve. Mix everything together really well with a wooden spoon.

5. Squeeze the mixture with your hands until a firm dough is formed. Make the dough into a large ball.

6. Sprinkle a clean work surface with a little flour. Then, roll out the ball of dough until it is ¼ of an inch thick.

If you hang cookies on a Christmas tree, don't eat them afterward.

7. Line the cookie sheet. Use a large cutter to press out lots of stars. Use a spatula to put them onto the sheet.

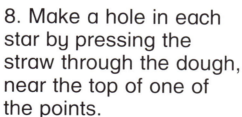

8. Make a hole in each star by pressing the straw through the dough, near the top of one of the points.

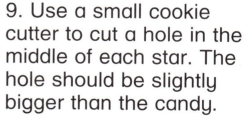

9. Use a small cookie cutter to cut a hole in the middle of each star. The hole should be slightly bigger than the candy.

10. Squeeze the leftover pieces of dough into a ball. Roll them out. Cut out more stars. Put them on the cookie sheet.

11. Drop a piece of candy into the hole in the middle of each star. Put the cookie sheet on the middle shelf of the oven.

12. Bake the shapes for twelve minutes, then take them out. Leave them on the cookie sheet until they are cold.

Snowmen and presents

To make lots of snowmen and presents, you will need:
9oz 'white' marzipan*
green, red and yellow food dyes
toothpicks

Coloring marzipan

Add a little powdered sugar if the marzipan gets too sticky.

1. Unwrap the marzipan. Then, put it on a plate and cut it into quarters. Put each quarter into a small bowl.

2. Add one drop of green food dye. Mix it in with your fingers. Continue until the marzipan is evenly colored.

3. Leave one quarter of the marzipan 'white'. Add red food dye to one quarter, and yellow to the other. Mix in the dye.

A snowman

Put the marzipan balls on a plate.

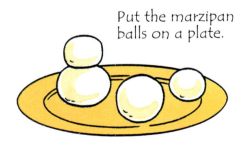

Press the ball with your thumb.

Cross the ends of the scarf.

1. Roll a piece of 'white' marzipan into a ball. Then, make a smaller ball. Press the smaller ball onto the larger one.

2. Roll a small ball of red marzipan. Press it to make a circle. Put it on the snowman's head. Put a tiny red ball on top.

3. Roll a thin strip of red marzipan. Wrap it around the snowman for a scarf. Press in a face with a toothpick.

* Marzipan contains ground nuts. Don't make these if you are allergic to nuts.

Ice a cake with butter icing (see pages 2-3) and decorate it with snowmen and presents.

A present

1. Roll a ball of red marzipan and put it on a work surface. Gently press the flat side of a knife down on the ball.

2. Turn the ball on its side and press it with the knife again. Keep on doing this until the ball becomes a cube.

3. Roll thin strips of green marzipan. Press them onto the cube, in a cross. Add two loops in the middle for a bow.

Iced gingerbread hearts

To make about 20 cookies, you will need:
2 cups flour
2 teaspoons of ground ginger
2 teaspoons of baking soda
½ cup butter or margarine, cut into chunks
¾ cup soft light brown sugar
¾ cup white sugar
1 medium egg
4 tablespoons of maple syrup
white writing icing
silver cake-decorating balls
large heart-shaped cookie cutter
2 greased cookie sheets

Heat the oven to 375°F, before you start.

You could wrap some cookies in tissue paper or cellophane twists, to give as a present.

1. Sift the flour, ground ginger and baking soda into a large bowl. Then, add the butter or margarine chunks.

2. Rub the butter or margarine into the flour with your fingers until it is like fine breadcrumbs. Stir in the sugar.

3. Break the egg into a small bowl, then add the syrup. Beat well with a fork, then stir the egg mixture into the flour.

4. Mix with a metal spoon until you make a dough. Sprinkle flour onto a work surface. Put the dough on it.

5. Stretch the dough by pushing it away from you. Fold it in half and repeat. Continue doing this until it is smooth.

6. Sprinkle more flour onto the work surface. Cut the dough in half. Roll out one half until it is about ¼ inch thick.

7. Use a cutter to cut out lots of hearts. Then, lift the hearts onto the greased cookie sheets with a spatula.

8. Roll out the rest of the dough and cut out more hearts. Put them on the cookie sheets, then put the sheets in the oven.

9. Bake the cookies for 12-15 minutes. They will turn golden brown. Carefully lift the cookie sheets from the oven.

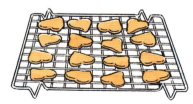

10. Leave the cookies on the sheets for about 5 minutes. Then, lift them onto a wire rack. Leave them to cool.

11. When the cookies are cold, draw lines across them with the icing. Cross some of the lines over each other.

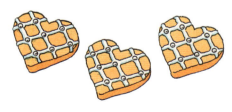

12. Leave the icing to harden a little. Then, push in a silver cake-decorating ball where the lines of icing cross.

Christmas tree cupcakes

To make 15 cupcakes, you will need:
1¼ cups self-rising flour
2 medium eggs
⅔ cup soft margarine
⅔ cup sugar
baking cups
2 muffin pans
candy for decorating

For the butter icing:
⅔ cup butter, softened
2½ cups powdered sugar, sifted
1 teaspoon of vanilla extract

Heat the oven to 375°F, before you start.

1. Break the eggs into a cup. Then, sift the flour through a sieve into a big bowl. Add the eggs, margarine and sugar.

2. Stir everything together with a wooden spoon. Continue until you get a smooth creamy mixture.

3. Put the baking cups in the muffin pans. Use a spoon to half-fill each baking cup with the cake mixture.

Stir it very quickly.

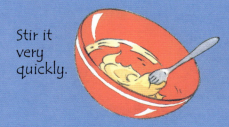

4. Bake the cakes for about 20 minutes and carefully take them out of the oven. Leave them on a rack to cool.

5. To make the icing, put the butter or margarine into a bowl and stir it with a fork. Continue until it is really creamy.

6. Add some of the powdered sugar to the butter and stir it in. Mix in the rest of the sugar, a little at a time.

7. Stir the lemon juice or vanilla extract into the mixture. Add a little more if the icing is very thick.

Arrange the cupcakes into a tree shape, like this.

8. Spread some butter icing on the top of each cupcake. Use candy to make different patterns on each one.

Use a flaky chocolate bar as a tree trunk.

Wrapping ideas

Tissue twists

1. Cut a square of tissue paper or thin cellophane. Then, put five or six cookies in the middle of the square.

2. Gather up the edges of the square. Tie a piece of ribbon around the tissue or cellophane, above the gift.

3. Decorate the paper with small stickers. You could also try wrapping cookies with two colors of paper or cellophane.

Wrapping candy

1. Cut a square of thin cellophane that is bigger than the candy, like this. Put the candy in the middle of the square.

Use a tiny piece of tape.

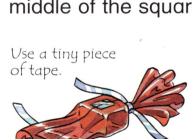

2. Wrap the candy in the cellophane and tape it. Tie pieces of ribbon around each end of the candy.

Gift boxes filled with candy and cookies make great presents.

Gift boxes

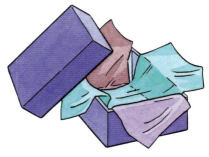

Paint the inside of a gift box silver or gold. When the paint is dry, fill the box with lots of shredded tissue paper.

Lay a piece of ribbon across the lid and tape it inside. Lay another piece across it. Decorate the lid with stickers.

Cut a piece of tissue paper that is a little bigger than the box. Cut pieces in other colors. Line the box.

Find out how to make gift tags on page 32.

Tags and ribbons

A gift tag

1. Draw a holly leaf shape with a white wax crayon or white candle. Brush bright paint all over the cardboard.

2. Carefully cut around the shape. Write a message on the back. Tape the end of the tag to a present.

Ribbon curls

Put your thumb here.

Pull this end.

1. Cut a piece of ribbon 10in. long. Cut more pieces of ribbon the same length.

2. Hold a piece of ribbon between your thumb and the blade of some closed scissors. Pull it firmly.

3. The ribbon curls up. Curl the other pieces of ribbon. Tape them to the middle of a box.

With thanks to the Sales department at EDC.

First published in 2001 by Usborne Publishing Ltd. Usborne House, 83-85 Saffron Hill, London EC1N 8RT, England. www.usborne.com